The Trenton Pickle Ordinance

The Trenton Pickle Ordinance

and other bonehead legislation

Compiled by

DICK HYMAN

With Cartoons by Bob Dunn

The Stephen Greene Press

BRATTLEBORO, VERMONT

PUBLISHED APRIL 1976
Second printing July 1976
Third printing November 1976
Fourth printing November 1977
Fifth printing January 1978
Sixth printing June 1978
Seventh printing August 1979
35,500 books in print

This book has been produced in the United States of America: designed by R. L. Dothard Associates, composed by American Book–Stratford Press, and printed and bound by The Book Press.

It is published by The Stephen Greene Press, Brattleboro, Vermont 05301

Library of Congress Cataloging in Publication Data

Main entry under title:

The Trenton pickle ordinance and other bonehead
   legislation.

   1. Law--Miscellanea. 2. Law--United States--
Popular works. I. Hyman, Dick, 1904-
Law   340'.0973   75-41874
ISBN 0-8289-0278-X

❦❦❦❦❦❦❦❦❦❦❦❦❦❦❦❦❦❦❦❦❦❦❦❦❦❦

The dogmas of the quiet past are inadequate to the stormy present . . . As our case is new, so must we think anew and act anew.

❦❦❦❦❦❦❦❦❦❦❦❦❦❦❦❦❦❦❦❦❦❦❦❦❦❦

Abraham Lincoln, in his message to Congress. December 1, 1862.

Foreword

by Bob Considine

We hold these Truths to be self-evident, that all Men are created equal, that they are endowed by their Creator with certain unalienable Rights, that among these are Life, Liberty, and the Pursuit of Happiness . . .

When Thomas Jefferson quilled those immortal words I wonder if he could have realized that one day the State of Idaho would pass a law making it illegal for a man to give his sweetheart a box of candy weighing less than fifty pounds. Doesn't this impede the Pursuit of Happiness?

Note: This Foreword was written by the late Bob Considine two weeks before his death on September 25, 1975.

The Founding Fathers figured they had put together a Declaration that would forever free Americans of the petty tyrannies of George III. Had they known when they signed the great document that some of their descendants would impose screwier laws on Americans than Nutty George ever dreamed of, they might have written him letters of apology.

For example, George never ordained (as did the Belvedere, California, Council) that "No dog shall be in a public place without its owner on a leash." In his balmiest moment, His Majesty never came up with anything as daft as the New York code that makes it illegal to shoot at a hare or jack-rabbit from a trolley car in transit.

The king would have hired a hundred thousand more Hessians, at five bucks a head, and vanquished General Washington's rag-tail rebels, if he had known that the city which was named after the Father of Our Country passed a law preventing horseback riders from fishing in the Potomac. Washington, D.C., has still another law which strikes at man's promised independence: no Washingtonian is allowed to fist-fight a bull!

Florida goes to extremes to thwart men's yearnings for Liberty. In Winter Garden there is a local ordinance which states flatly that it is a crime for a man to escape from the hoose-gow.

The British Crown never horsed around with the people of Georgia quite as outrageously as did freed Georgians themselves. You can get locked up in Georgia for slapping a friend on the back, or beating your rug in a town square, or saying "Oh, boy!" in the town of Jonesboro.

The legal mind regards mules with a special reverence. You can't light a fire under one in Ohio. You can't kick one in Arizona. Other states list laws which deny equal rights to certain others of God's creatures. In Berea, Kentucky, all animals on the streets after dark must wear red tail-lights. Lions are barred from Maryland theaters, and hens cannot cackle at will in the residential sections of Kenilworth, Illinois.

The language of a Texas statute suggests

that when two trains meet at a crossing each shall come to a full stop, "and neither shall proceed until the other has gone." In Glendale, Arizona, you can wind up in the can if you are caught backing up your car. Idaho makes second-class citizens of all its men folk. If they are cursed by women, *the men* are to be fined for any disturbance that results.

Barbers at Waterloo, Nebraska, must feel as lucky as Napoleon did at that other Waterloo: they are forbidden by law to eat onions between 7 A.M. and 7 P.M. Stay clear of Portland, Oregon, if you have an itch—or an urgent need —to roller skate into a public rest room. When in Spartanburg, South Carolina, avoid, if possible, eating watermelons in the Magnolia Street Cemetery. Check your bean shooter in a locker at the airport on your next trip to Arkansas— they're *verboten*.

If your favorite headache powder isn't curing you of a hangover any longer, don't expect to find fast, fast relief in Trout Creek, Utah. Local pharmacists may no longer sell you a treasured remedy—gunpowder. And, speaking of illegal uses of gunpowder, did those Minutemen at Lexington and Concord two hundred years ago know that Massachusetts forbids possession of more than four hundred pounds of gunpowder at one time?

Getting back to Jefferson, a fastidious and romantic man, I wonder if he could have comprehended that two centuries after the Declaration there's still a law on the books in his own Virginia which forbids bathtubs inside the house (they must be kept in the yard, the law states), and that in Norfolk freedom of speech is even now suppressed, to the point that you can't so much as make cracks about the local firemen.

Let's have a rewrite, Tom.

Bob Considine

Publisher's Note

In the evolution of Western Law, there are few great milestones:

The Ten Commandments——
The Code of Justinian——
Magna Carta——
The Napoleonic Code——
And now . . . **The Trenton Pickle Ordinance.**

As it begins its third century, the United States, heretofore known only for such trivial contributions to legal science as the federal Constitution and the works of Mr. Justice Holmes, has at last produced a classic—the volume now in hand.

Compiled by the pre-eminent (perhaps the sole) authority in its field, this authoritative compendium has a dual purpose. It preserves, and dedicates to the future, a body of legislation both grand and wise, the precious fruit of elevated legal minds in every section of the Republic.

Less monumentally, it offers to the ordinary citizen a guide through the toils of the law—a guide the need for which will not be doubted by any unfortunate who has carelessly eaten a watermelon in the community of Hammond, Indiana, or spat into the wind in Sault Sainte Marie (Michigan).

The Publisher wishes to note, for the benefit of legal scholars yet unborn, that several of the laws collected here have been published in other books. For this no apology is to be expected. Moses would not have forborne to announce his First Commandment simply because it had turned up on someone else's Table, too.

The laws in this work that have appeared elsewhere are properly a part of the American Legal Heritage. The strictures against unrestrained giggling (Montana) and pouring pickle juice on the car tracks (Rhode Island) can take their places with the Bill of Rights, the Dartmouth College Case, and the Dred Scott Decision, as elements of the living tradition of jurisprudence that is the common trust of all Americans.

Castle W. Freeman, Jr.
for the Publisher

Author's Note

It all began forty years ago, during a discussion I had with a judge in the little town of Jasper, Alabama. He told me of a law in his community that read "since the Alabama husband is accountable for his wife's misbehavior, he has the legal right to chastise her with a stick no larger than the thumb. . . ." My curiosity was so thoroughly aroused that when I returned to New York City I sought and got special permission to research the subject of curious laws in the library of the New York Bar Association. The revelations of that Alabama judge, together with my insatiable appetite for research, led to the idea of a newspaper feature on loony laws. The feature, called "It's the Law," ran in Hearst's New York **Sunday Mirror** at first, and later appeared as a cartoon feature in the **American Magazine** for twenty-two years until the magazine folded in 1956.

Over the years, I have accumulated a file of some two thousand bonehead laws, of which the six hundred best (or worst) are collected here. My mail has brought in hundreds of letters from cities, towns and villages in all fifty states citing crazy laws and enclosing copies of the printed laws.

Many of the laws collected here go back to the horse-and-buggy era but have never been rescinded, in spite of their all-too-obvious obsolescence. Although a few of the laws have by now been canceled out by their states, most remain on the books.

Dick Hyman

Actors

In Boston, it is against the law to kiss an actor during a stage performance.

Airplanes

Alaska says it's against the law to look at a moose from an airplane.

Thomasville, North Carolina, prohibits airplanes from flying over the town on Sundays during the hours between 11 A.M. and 1 P.M.

Alcoholic Beverages

An Alabama law makes it illegal for anyone to own or sell anything that "tastes like, smells like, or looks like beer."

In Indiana, motorists can be tested for alcoholic breath against their will under a law that "after the breath leaves the body it ceases to be the property of the person from whom it came."

It is unlawful to drink beer in your underwear in Cushing, Oklahoma.

In Cold Springs, Pennsylvania, liquor may not be sold to a married man except with the written consent of his wife.

A law in Greenville, South Carolina, says that whiskey cannot be bought or sold unless the sun is shining.

And it's against the law to own a copy of the *Encyclopaedia Britannica* in Texas—because it contains a liquor formula.

In Cartersville, Georgia, you must be inside your house and seated to drink a bottle of beer.

Maine law states that you can sell beer to men only while they remain standing.

Alligators

Corpus Christi, Texas, makes it illegal to raise alligators in your home.

It is against the law to molest an alligator in Miami.

Animals (Unspecified)

In Miami, it is forbidden to go around imitating animals.

Montana passed a law providing that if you catch a fur-bearing animal and tattoo your name on it, the animal thereafter belongs to you.

Arkansas

It is illegal to mispronounce the name of the State of Arkansas in that state.

3 §

Automobiles

Automobiles in Detroit must not be decorated with pennants, under penalty of the law.

In Nebraska, a motorist must send up warning red rockets and Roman candles at night when he approaches a horse. He must throw a scenic tarpaulin over his car to conceal it from the horse. Also, he must take his machine apart and hide the parts in the grass if the tarpaulin doesn't soothe the horse.

It is against Decatur, Illinois, law to drive a car without a steering gear.

A California law forbids a woman to drive a car while she is dressed in a housecoat.

In Emporia, Kansas, when an automobile approaches the city, the car must stop at the city limits and a member of the party in the car must precede it through the city afoot and warn the people that they are going to drive through, so people can get their horses out of the street.

In Memphis, it is against the law for a woman to drive a car unless there is a man either running or walking in front of the car waving a red flag to warn approaching motorists and pedestrians.

Also in Tennessee, it is illegal to drive any car while asleep.

In Glendale, Arizona, it is against the law for a car to back up.

Cleveland law forbids you to operate a motor vehicle while sitting in another person's lap.

Another Ohio statute prohibits motorists in Youngstown from running out of gas.

Minneapolis makes red automobiles unlawful.

Across the river in St. Paul, a driver meeting a horse-drawn vehicle must get out and help the driver of the horse to pass the auto.

Philadelphia says you can't operate an automobile on the city streets unless it has been inspected—by the Bureau of Boiler Inspection.

In Rutland, Vermont, it is illegal to permit your car to backfire.

Washington law says that a driver of a car not equipped with ash trays, is liable to a two-hundred-dollar fine.

It is against the law to drive an auto bare-footed or with bedroom slippers on in Alabama.

Legislation proposed in the Illinois State Legislature, May, 1907: "Speed upon county roads will be limited to ten miles an hour unless the motorist sees a bailiff who does not appear to have had a drink in 30 days, when the driver will be permitted to make what he can."

Evanston, Illinois, makes it unlawful to change clothes in an automobile with the curtains drawn, except in case of fire.

It is the law in Lake Forest, Illinois, that

every auto on the street shall be preceded by a bicycle.

Also in Illinois, Macomb makes it illegal for a car to impersonate a wolf.

In Corning, Iowa, it's a misdemeanor for a man to ask his wife to ride in any motor vehicle.

New York has a law forbidding blind men from driving automobiles.

In Milwaukee an ordinance says that no automobile can be parked over two hours unless hitched to a horse.

In another Wisconsin town, the court sagely noted that "Much advice and many suggestions to the driver by one sitting in the rear seat (in this case, the wife) are not conducive to the best management of the car."

Michigan law forbids stepping into the path of a moving vehicle; doing so constitutes a traffic hazard.

Another Michigan law, in Grand Rapids,

provides a fine for "embracing or being embraced while a car is in motion."

Baby Carriages

In Rockville, Maryland, it is against the law to push baby carriages down a sidewalk two abreast.

In Roderfield, West Virginia, only babies are allowed to ride in baby carriages.

It is unlawful for a mother to roll a baby carriage on the streets of Tupelo, Mississippi.

Baby Sitters

It is against Altoona, Pennsylvania, law for a baby sitter to clean out his or her employer's ice box.

Back-slapping

In Georgia, it is against the law to slap a man on the back.

Bakeries

Massachusetts law states that it is a crime to lounge on shelves in a bakery.

Balloons

The District of Columbia has a law forbidding you to exert pressure on a balloon and thereby cause a whistling sound on the streets.

Barbers & Barbershops

In Fitchburg, Massachusetts, barbers are not allowed to carry combs in back of their ears.

It is an old state law in Alabama that no person can sleep all night in a barbershop.

And in Erie, Pennsylvania, it is against the law to fall asleep while having your hair cut in a barber's chair.

Milwaukee law prohibits barbers from using powder puffs while practicing barbering.

It is unlawful for a barber to advertise his prices in Georgia.

But in Baton Rouge, Louisiana, a bill was introduced in the state house of representatives fixing a twenty-five-cent ceiling on haircuts for bald men.

Omaha, Nebraska, makes it against the law for a barber to shave a man's chest.

Hair, neck and shaving brushes were outlawed in the barbershops of the District of Columbia.

It is illegal in Elkhart, Indiana, for a barber to threaten to cut off a youngster's ears.

Barbers in Waterloo, Nebraska, are forbidden by law to eat onions between 7 A.M. and 7 P.M.

Barrel-rolling

A Pensacola, Florida, law prohibits rolling a barrel in the streets.

Bartenders

In Mazama, Washington, bartenders are subject to fines if they listen in on conversations between customers.

Baseball

In Marengo, Iowa, the law says that no more than twenty-seven persons shall participate in a baseball game.

In Muskogee, Oklahoma, there is an old city ordinance that states that no baseball team shall be allowed to hit the ball over the fence or out of the ball park.

A Portsmouth, Ohio, law ranks baseball players with "vagrants, thieves and other suspicious characters."

Bathing Suits

Kentucky forbids persons to appear on the

streets of any town or village in bathing dress without police protection.

Another Kentucky law prohibits making dates on the streets by persons in bathing suits.

In Rochester, Michigan, anyone bathing in public must have his or her bathing suit inspected by a police officer.

Baths & Bathtubs

According to Kentucky state law, every person must take a bath at least once a year.

But an old Boston law states that no one shall take more than one bath per week.

Another Boston statute forbids a person to take a bath unless he has a written prescription from a medical doctor.

In Minneapolis it is against the law to install any bathtub other than one with legs.

It is illegal in Florida for one to bathe in a bathtub without wearing a bathing suit or some sort of apparel.

§ 14

It is a violation of Arkansas law to make a false oath in order to obtain a free bath in Hot Springs.

Montgomery, Alabama, makes it illegal to bathe in the courthouse square fountain.

In Morrisville, Vermont, the law requires that anyone desirous of taking a bath must first secure a permit from the Board of Selectmen.

A bill introduced in the Wisconsin legislature provided that "every proprietor of a lumber camp must supply an individual bath tub for each lumberjack in his employ."

Only one person may take a bath in a tub at one time, according to another Wisconsin law.

Virginia law forbids bathtubs in the house; tubs must be kept in the yard.

Pennsylvania forbids singing in the bathtub, and prohibits the sale of bathtubs.

And in Mohave County, Arizona, a decree

declares that anyone caught stealing soap must wash himself with it until it is all used up.

Bean Shooters

In Arkansas, bean shooters are prohibited. Any person found using a bean shooter or similar implement shall be deemed guilty of a misdemeanor.

Bean Shooters (Concealed)

Wichita, Kansas, City Ordinance 349: "Any person who shall in the city of Wichita use or carry concealed or unconcealed any bean snapper or like article shall, upon conviction, be fined."

Beards

New York City law states that all whiskers

worn in public by Santa Clauses must be fire-proof.

In Anchorage, Alaska, it is the law that every year all male residents shall raise beards from January 5th to the middle of February, when a celebration called the Fur Rendezvous is held.

Beards more than two and a half feet long are forbidden by law in Altoona, Pennsylvania.

Bears

Missouri law says it is illegal to carry an uncaged bear down a highway.

In Virginia, it is against the law to drive or lead an unconfined bear along the street.

It is against Youngstown, Ohio, law to keep a bear without a license.

Alaska says you cannot disturb a grizzly bear to take its picture.

It is unlawful in Maine to exhibit bears unless you are an authorized menagerie.

Bees

Michigan state law regulates the transportation of bees.

In Lawrence, Kansas, you can't carry bees around in your hat on the city streets.

Bicycles

It is illegal for anyone to ride his or her bicycle backwards on the main streets of Forgan, Oklahoma.

In Santa Ana, California, it is unlawful to pass a fire truck while riding a bicycle.

Bird Baths (Public)

Duncan, Oklahoma, says it is against the law

for anyone to wash clothing in a public drinking fountain or bird bath.

Birds

The Utah State Code holds that birds have the right of way on public highways.

Biting

In Rumford, Maine, it's against the law to bite your landlord.

Blasphemy

Kentucky law states that a fine of one dollar must be paid for every cuss word used in public.

Boats

In San Francisco, it is illegal to dump or

discard a boat or ark on any submerged street.

In Fairfield, Alabama, it is against the law to go down Gary Avenue in a rowboat.

Bologna

Memphis law prohibits the sale of bologna on Sunday.

Bribery

The Virginia Code (1930) has a statute: "To prohibit corrupt practices or bribery by any person other than candidates."

Bridges

Providence, Rhode Island, law forbids you to leap over local bridges.

Bronx Cheers

A New York City judge ruled that if two women behind you at the movies insist on discussing the probable outcome of the film, you have the right to turn around and blow a Bronx cheer at them.

Buffalo

Newton, Kansas, forbids the driving of buffalo through the streets.

Busses

In Bristol, Connecticut, anyone found writing on a bus is fined twenty dollars; anyone writing inside a bus is fined fifty dollars or more.

Florida has a law prohibiting the transporting of livestock on school busses.

Cabbage

An Ocean City, New Jersey, law forbids the sale of cabbage on the Sabbath.

Calendar Art

In Texas, ladies on calendars hanging in public saloons must be decently clad.

Camels

Galveston, Texas, makes it illegal for camels to wander unattended in the streets.

It is against the law to drive a camel on the public highways of Nevada.

Carpet Beating

Carpet beating in the public square in Savannah, Georgia, is punishable by law.

Cats

Fights between cats and dogs are prohibited by statute in Barber, North Carolina.

In Sterling, Colorado, it is unlawful to allow a pet cat to run loose without a tail-light.

A Topeka, Kansas, law limits any household to a maximum possession of five cats.

In Cresskill, New Jersey, all cats must wear not one but three bells to warn birds of their whereabouts.

International Falls, Minnesota, forbids cats to chase dogs up telephone poles.

Cattle

There is a state law prohibiting the blindfolding of cows on Arkansas public highways.

Washington, D.C., says that no one shall engage in a pugilistic encounter with a bull.

Cemeteries

Oklahoma states that it is against the law to rob a bird's nest in a public cemetery.

In Bath, New York, any person who resorts to a burial ground with "abandoned women" is subject to a fine of fifty dollars.

It is unlawful in Muncie, Indiana, to carry fishing tackle into the cemetery.

Chewing Gum

In Cleveland, it is unlawful to leave chewing gum in public places.

Chickens

In Kenilworth, Illinois, a rooster must step back three hundred feet from any residence if he wishes to crow. Hens that wish to cackle must step two hundred feet back from any residence.

If you let a chicken's head dangle you are breaking one of the ordinances of the Columbus, Georgia, city code.

In Quitman, Georgia, it is against the law for any chicken to cross any road within the city limits.

Norfolk, Virginia, says hens cannot lay eggs before 8 A.M. and after 4 P.M.

Idaho law requires a person to have a permit from the sheriff to buy a chicken in the state after dark.

Children

Colorado Statutes Annotated, Section 150, Chapter 78: "No maternity hospital shall receive a child without its mother except in cases of emergency."

In Winston-Salem, North Carolina, it is

against the law for children under seven years of age to go to college.

A Blue Earth, Minnesota, law declares that no child under the age of twelve may talk over the telephone unless accompanied by a parent.

It is unlawful for parents in the District of Columbia to allow children under fourteen years of age to be employed either as a rope-walker, an acrobat or a contortionist.

Another D.C. order makes it against the law for small boys to throw stones, at any time, at any place.

Cigar Butts

New York state law makes it illegal for children to collect old cigar butts.

Clam Chowder

In Massachusetts, it is forbidden to put tomatoes in clam chowder.

Coal

It is unlawful to throw coal at another person in Harlan, Kentucky—if the size of the lump exceeds three inches.

Commerce

In Paducah, Kentucky, it is against the law for a merchant to drag or pull a person from the street for the purpose of making a sale.

Concealed Weapons

In Seattle, you can't carry a concealed weapon that is over six feet in length.

Concerts & Musical Entertainments

In Milwaukee it is unlawful to play a fife and drum on the street for the purpose of attracting attention.

Females are not allowed to play in orchestras in Connecticut after 10 P.M.

Confetti

San Francisco has an ordinance banning picking up used confetti to throw again.

Cookie Jars

In Joliet, Illinois, it is against the law to put cake in a cookie jar.

Cooks

There is a state law in Florida that forbids you to hire away your neighbor's cook.

Cornflakes

It is against the law to sell cornflakes on Sunday in Columbus, Ohio.

Corsets

An Iowa law states that women are not allowed to wear corsets. (When this law was first passed years ago, men were appointed as corset inspectors. Their duty was to poke women in the ribs to see if they were wearing corsets.)

In Norfolk, Virginia, a girl cannot attend a public dance without wearing a corset.

Costumes

It is a criminal offense in Massachusetts to wear a costume while collecting a debt.

Courtship & Marriage

In Nebraska, a husband is justified in slapping his wife if he can show that it was necessary to do so in order to compel her to go out for a ride for the benefit of her health.

If a Dixie, Idaho, lady berates her husband in public causing a crowd to collect, the husband shall be fined.

Also in Idaho, the legislature passed a law making it illegal for a man to give his sweetheart a box of candy weighing less than fifty pounds.

Whitesville, Delaware, deems it disorderly conduct for a woman to offer a marriage proposal during a Leap Year.

It is against the law in Portland, Oregon, for anyone to perform a wedding in a skating rink or theater.

In Cleveland, you can't get married in a bathing suit.

There is a Kentucky law that forbids a housewife to move the furniture in her home without her husband's consent.

Another Kentucky law prohibits women from marrying the same man four times.

A Tennessee man cannot divorce his wife unless he leaves her ten pounds of dried beans, five pounds of dried apples, one side of meat and enough yarn to knit her own stockings for twelve months.

In 1893, Pennsylvania passed a law providing protection for husbands: "A husband is not guilty of desertion when the wife rents his room to a boarder and crowds him out of the house."

The same state says that a woman who meets another woman who is playing up to the first woman's husband may flog that woman providing that she uses anything but her hand.

Alabama husbands have the legal right to chastize their wives with "sticks no larger than the thumb."

But in Tennessee, a man can beat his wife if he uses nothing larger than a broom handle.

Under Virginia law a man has the right to curse and abuse his wife either in his house or outside, provided he does so in a low voice.

§ 32

It is against Connecticut law for a man to write love letters to a girl whose mother has forbidden him to see her.

Vermont says that a woman cannot walk down the street on a Sunday unless her husband walks twenty paces behind her with a musket on his shoulder.

In Lebanon, Tennessee, a husband can't kick his wife out of bed, even though her feet are cold; a wife, however, can kick her husband out of bed anytime, without giving a reason.

In Oregon, it is unlawful for a college student to pin his fraternity badge on one who is not a member of that fraternity.

There is an old Michigan law that says a husband owns his wife's clothes, and if she leaves him he can follow her on the street and remove every article of said clothing.

Another Michigan law states that married couples must live together or be imprisoned.

A New York court held that a strong desire to marry on the part of a man is not *prima facie* evidence of insanity.

Cowboy Boots

In Blythe, California, a city ordinance declares that a person must own at least two cows before he is permitted to wear cowboy boots in public.

And a Madisonville, Texas, law requires persons to own at least two cows before they are allowed to tuck their trousers legs into the tops of their cowboy boots.

Cowboys

In Phoenix, Arizona, cowboys cannot walk through hotel lobbies wearing spurs.

Cravats & Neckties

Minneapolis law declares that no male dancer

shall enter upon any public dance floor in the city without wearing some form of cravat.

In Groton, Connecticut, the law asserts that "any utterances from a man in a bow tie are not to be credited."

Crockery

Florida law states that you are not allowed to crack more than three dishes per day, or chip the edges of more than four cups and/or saucers.

Cuspidors

In Pittsburgh, cuspidors are not allowed in jury boxes; they offend the sensibilities of female jurors.

It is unlawful for Hammond, Indiana, tobacco users to miss a spittoon.

In Plant City, Florida, the law requires that all barber shops be provided with cuspidors "of an impervious material."

Dancing

A Stockton, California, law of 1926 makes it illegal to wiggle while dancing.

In Los Angeles there is an ordinance forbidding infants to dance in public halls.

By statute in Bellingham, Washington, a woman must not take more than three steps backward while dancing.

Monroe, Utah, requires that daylight be visible between dancing couples.

An Iowa City law prohibits the following steps in public dance halls: the Charleston, the Grizzly Bear, the Bunny Hug, the Texas Tommy, and the Turkey Trot.

Forbidden in Belt, Montana, are: the Tango,
the Duck Wobble, the Angle Worm Wiggle, and
the Kangaroo Glide.

Dandelions

It is against the law in Pueblo, Colorado, to
raise or permit a dandelion to grow within the
city limits.

Debtors

The New York Penal Code states that anyone who arrests a dead man for debt is guilty
of a misdemeanor.

Diapers

In Massachusetts, it is unlawful to deliver
diapers on Sunday, regardless of emergencies.

Disorderly Conduct

All persons who shall be found at any time underneath sidewalks shall be guilty of disorderly conduct in Florida.

Doctors & Dentists

In Jamestown, New York, it is illegal for a dentist to hypnotize a patient before an extraction.

An ordinance in South Foster, Rhode Island, provides that a dentist who extracts the wrong tooth must have a corresponding tooth pulled by the village blacksmith, or pay a fine.

It is against Ohio law to call a doctor a "horse doctor"—even if he is one.

Dog Catchers

In Duncan, Oklahoma, it is illegal to resist, abuse or insult the dog catcher.

A law passed in Denver in 1936 says that the dog catcher must notify dogs of impounding by posting, for three consecutive days, a notice on a tree in the city park and along a public road running through said park.

In Pender, Nebraska, the office of dog catcher may not be held by a Chinaman.

Dog Fights

Idaho state law prohibits persons from participating in dog fights.

Lockport, Illinois, stipulates that anyone will be fined who starts a dog fight by word or gesture.

Under a Lexington, Missouri, law of 1911, it is forbidden to "incite" a dog fight anywhere on a public thoroughfare.

Dogs

You can't take a French poodle to an opera house in Chicago.

In Albany, Oregon, a beggar may not have a dog for a partner.

Hartford, Connecticut, makes it illegal to educate dogs.

There is a Massachusetts law requiring all dogs to have their hind legs tied during the month of April.

In Paulding, Ohio, a policeman may bite a dog to quiet him.

Boston makes it illegal to keep a dog more than ten inches in height.

Dogs in Denver are not entitled to transfers on the tramways; also, they must pay full fare.

A Belvedere, California, City Council order reads: "No dog shall be in a public place without its master on a leash."

Double Parking

In Minneapolis, people who double park can

§ 40

be put on the chain gang and fed on bread and water.

Doughnuts

An Oak Park, Illinois, ordinance forbids frying more than a hundred doughnuts in a single day.

Dress Dummies

Dressing a store-window figure in public is prohibited in Atlanta. Window-dressers must pull down a shade during the robing and disrobing of their mannikins.

Dresses

Women in Joliet, Illinois, can be jailed for trying on more than six dresses in one store.

Drinking Fountains

In Garden City, Kansas, the law says you can't drink from the public drinking fountains.

Ears

It is against the law of Hawaii for a person to insert pennies in the ear.

Eating-places

A Chicago law forbids eating in a place that is on fire.

Eggs

Iowa state law makes it illegal to have a rotten egg in your possession.

In Rawson, Ohio, an ordinance forbids

throwing rotten eggs on the premises of another.

Elephants

San Francisco prohibits elephants from strolling down Market Street unless they are on a leash.

Faces

Pocatello, Idaho, City Ordinance 1100 prohibits frowns, grimaces, scowls, threatening and lowering looks, and gloomy and depressed facial appearances generally, all of which reflect unfavorably upon the reputation of the city.

In Normal, Illinois, it is against the law to make faces at dogs.

Trenton, New Jersey, makes it illegal for a

sheep herder to wear a false face or disguise while driving sheep over the streets.

In Garfield County, Montana, it is ordered that no one shall draw funny faces on window shades.

California law states that wrestlers may not make faces during the practice of their art.

It is unlawful to wear a false face in Denver.

Fan Dancers

In Montana, a fan dancer in a place where liquor is sold must wear a costume weighing at least three pounds, two ounces.

Feather Dusters

In Clarendon, Texas, it is illegal to dust any public buildings with a feather duster.

Texas again: Borger outlaws throwing confetti, rubber balls, feather dusters, whips or quirts, and explosive firecrackers of any kind.

Portland, Maine, makes it illegal to tickle a girl under the chin with a feather duster.

Portland, Oregon, for its part, prohibits shaking a feather duster in another person's face.

Feet

A Massachusetts state law forbids cooling one's feet by hanging them out the window.

Ohio law forbids sticking your feet out of your car door to enjoy the breezes.

Finger Bowls

It is against the law in Omaha for different people to use the same finger bowl.

Firearms

Georgia law provides that it is a misdemeanor for any citizen to attend church worship on Sunday unless he is equipped with a rifle and it is loaded.

It is unlawful in Woonsocket, Rhode Island, to remove icicles from buildings by taking pot-shots at them with a gun or rifle.

Minors in Kansas City, Missouri, are not allowed to purchase cap pistols; they can buy shotguns freely, however.

It is contrary to Pennsylvania law to discharge a gun, cannon, revolver or other explosive weapon at a wedding.

In Wichita, Kansas, a father cannot frighten his daughter's boy friend with a gun.

Firemen

An ordinance in Hiawatha, Kansas, gives

§ 46

firemen the right of way on sidewalks when they are going to and from work.

The South Norfolk, Virginia, council passed an ordinance forbidding anyone to make critical remarks about the methods employed by local firemen while they are in the act of fighting a fire.

In Racine, Wisconsin, it is illegal to wake a fireman when he is alseep.

An old Nebraska law forbids firemen to play checkers.

In Fort Madison, Iowa, the fire department is required to practice fire fighting for fifteen minutes before attending a fire.

A Zeigler, Illinois, law states that only the first four firemen reaching a fire will be paid for their services.

Fish

In Salt Lake City, Utah, you cannot give

away a fish on a Sunday or on a legal holiday.

Fishing

According to state law in Maine, fishermen must take off their hats to the game warden.

It is illegal to fish on the Chicago breakwater in pajamas.

In Berkeley, California, it is against the law to be caught smoking, or with matches in your possession, while out fishing.

Oregon state law forbids the use of canned corn in fishing.

Dynamite cannot be used for the purpose of catching fish in Illinois.

In the District of Columbia, it is illegal to catch fish while on horseback.

Kansas says you can't catch fish with your bare hands.

To catch a whale in the inland waters of the State of Oklahoma is contrary to law.

Foot-tapping

New Hampshire law forbids you to tap your foot, nod your head, or in any way keep time to music in a tavern, restaurant or café.

Fortune Telling & Allied Arts

It is state law in New Jersey that any person who practices witchcraft or sorcery to discover lost or stolen goods may be taken to court and found guilty of a misdemeanor.

In Georgia, no Confederate soldier may tell fortunes or practice palmistry without first paying a tax.

It is illegal in Arkansas to engage in the business of fortune telling, or to practice the avocation of phrenology or craniology.

§ 50

Frogs

In Boston, it is unlawful to hold frog-jumping contests in night clubs.

A person may not persuade another to kill a frog for him in West Virginia.

Frogs are prohibited from croaking after 11 P.M. in Memphis.

It is illegal to disturb a bullfrog in Hayden, Arizona.

Fruits & Vegetables

Waynesboro, Virginia, prohibits anyone from eating fruit or nuts on the steps of a church.

It is contrary to the law of California to peel an orange in a hotel room.

Yuma, Arizona, decrees that persons caught stealing citrus fruits will be given a dose of castor oil.

There is a Michigan state law that no fruit peddler may coat his fruit with varnish to bring out its beauty.

In Dansville, Michigan, it is illegal to toss spoiled vegetables at an entertainer.

It is unlawful to plant vegetables in California cemeteries.

Funerals

Massachusetts law once banned excessive eating at funerals.

Funny Stories

Nicholas County, West Virginia, forbids clergymen to tell funny stories from the pulpit.

Garbage & Garbage Cans

Brattleboro, Vermont, requires all junk dealers to be United States citizens.

It is against the law to kick a garbage can in New Orleans.

In Alabama it is illegal to sit on a garbage can.

El Paso, Texas, has a law forbidding the throwing of faded bouquets into garbage cans.

Gargling

It is against the law to gargle in public in Louisiana.

Geese

In California it is forbidden for anyone to pick feathers from live geese.

A McDonald, Ohio, ordinance prohibits marching geese down the streets of the village.

Giggling

Unrestrained giggling is forbidden on the streets of Helena, Montana.

Giraffes

Atlanta makes it against the law to tie a giraffe to a telephone pole or street lamp.

Glancing

In Alabama, it is unlawful for a man to glance in any place not his own that is occupied by a female person.

Goats

Birmingham, Alabama, Ordinances, Section 135: "It shall be unlawful to drive within the corporate limits of the city a wagon or other vehicle, drawn by goats for the purpose of advertising any article, trade or occupation."

In California it is illegal for a dog to worry a cashmere goat.

It is against the law in Chaseville, New York, to drive a goat past a church on Sunday "in a ridiculous fashion."

Minneapolis forbids keeping goats in an apartment, though mules may thus be kept.

Goldfish

Seattle passed an ordinance that states that goldfish could ride the city busses in bowls only if they kept still.

Golf

In Albany, New York, you cannot play golf in the streets.

Grocery Carts

Babies in Los Angeles are forbidden to ride in a grocery pushcart with food their mothers have been buying.

Gunpowder

Pharmacists in Trout Creek, Utah, may not sell gunpowder as a headache cure.

In Boston, an ordinance prohibits anyone from possessing more than four hundred pounds of gunpowder at one time.

Hair

In Louisiana, it's the law that everything that has hair on its back must be dipped.

Haircutting

Minnesota makes it against the law for you

to cut your friends' or neighbors' hair without a license.

Hairdressers

It is against the law for a woman to give a man a permanent wave in Lindenhurst, New York.

Another New York law forbids baldheaded men to visit beauty shops for the purpose of having their hair regrown.

Hatpins

A Secaucus, New Jersey, law of 1898 reads: "Any person who shall wear in a public place any device or thing attached to her head, hair, headgear or hat, which device or thing is capable of lacerating the flesh of any other person with whom it may come in contact and which is not sufficiently guarded against the possibility of so doing, shall be adjudged a disorderly person."

Hats & Headgear

Fargo, North Dakota, law requires young women to remove their hats while dancing.

In Owensboro, Kentucky, it is illegal for a woman to buy a new hat without her husband trying it on first.

Montgomery, Alabama, makes it against the law to walk down the street with a sheet over your head.

Heels

Women in Utah must remember that a state law prohibits heels more than 1½ inches high.

High Water

The Arkansas Legislature passed a law that

states that the Arkansas River can rise no further than to the Main Street Bridge in Little Rock.

Hippopotamuses

A Los Angeles ordinance forbids a person to have a hippopotamus in his possession.

Hoops

It is against the law for anyone to roll a hoop within the city limits of Triadelphia, West Virginia.

Hoop Skirts

In Grand Haven, Michigan, no person shall throw an abandoned hoop skirt into any street or on any sidewalk, under penalty of a five dollar fine for each offense.

Horned Toads

No live horned toads may be taken out of the State of New Mexico except with the special permission of the Governor.

Horns

In Russell, Kansas, it is against the law to have a musical car horn.

And in Atlanta, law forbids diaper service trucks from having horns that play "Rock-A-Bye-Baby."

Horror Films

A Glendale, California, ordinance permits horror films to be shown only on Mondays, Tuesdays or Wednesdays.

Horses

In Wilbur, Washington, it is against the law

for a person to ride upon the streets on an ugly horse.

A Fountain Inn, South Carolina, law requires horses to wear pants at all times.

And Ft. Lauderdale, Florida, stipulates that all horses must be equipped with horns and tail-lights.

In Hillsboro, Oregon, it is unlawful to allow a horse to ride around in the back seat of your car.

Virginia makes it illegal for any person to willfully and negligently permit any unhaltered horse of the age of one year or more to ac-company him into any place of public worship.

According to Minnesota state law, if a horse is frightened by the noise an automobile makes after cranking, the owner of the car is responsi-ble for any damage the horse may do.

Horses are forbidden to eat fire hydrants in Marshalltown, Iowa.

Horseshoe-pitching

In Ohio, if you ignore an orator on Decoration Day to such an extent as to publicly play croquet or pitch horseshoes within one mile of the speaker's stand, you can be fined twenty-five dollars.

House-burning

Jackson, Mississippi, orders that if you want to burn down your house, you must first remove the top.

Humming

Cicero, Illinois, prohibits humming on public streets on Sundays.

Hunting & Shooting

In Ouray, Colorado, it is illegal to hunt elk on Main Street.

Los Angeles law forbids hunting moths under a street light.

It is against the law in Florida to hunt or kill deer while in swimming.

In Tennessee, you can't shoot any game other than whales from a moving automobile.

Hunting with a rifle is permitted in Norfolk County, Virginia—providing the hunter is fifteen feet off the ground.

In Cleveland, it is illegal to catch mice without a hunting license.

Frankfort, Kentucky, makes it against the law to shoot off a policeman's tie.

Kansas law prohibits shooting rabbits from a motorboat.

In Ft. Huachuca, Arizona, hunting buffalo on the parade ground is against the law.

New York City says you can't shoot rabbits from the rear of a Third Avenue streetcar—when the car is in motion.

It is against Michigan law to take waterfowl by means, aid, or use of cattle, horses, or mules.

If you meet a man in North Dakota who is wanted for a felony, and he refuses to accompany you to the police station, you are legally entitled to shoot him.

Ice Cream

No Cleveland peddlar of frozen desserts may cry his wares in a loud voice or use more than a soft chime.

Insects

The laws of New York City state that any person who fails to step on an insect using a public thoroughfare is liable to a fifty-dollar fine.

Kirkland, Illinois, law forbids bees to fly over the village or through any of its streets.

Insults

Nobody in Youngstown, Ohio, can lawfully abuse the Mayor aloud—not even taxpayers.

Intoxication

It is against the law in Oklahoma to get a fish drunk.

Hickory, North Carolina, says that drunken driving means steering an automobile with motor on or off.

According to the Code of Iowa (1939), pretended intoxication is just as much in violation of the law as actual intoxication.

Also in Iowa, Council Bluffs says it is illegal for an intoxicated person to either climb a tree or play baseball.

In Chicago there is a law against a person riding a bicycle while drunk.

A Missouri court ruled that "It is the inalienable right of the citizen to get drunk."

Itching Powder

It is illegal to sell sneezing powder, itching powder, or bombs, to anyone under the age of twenty-one in Jacksonville, Florida.

Juggling

In Hood River, Oregon, you can't juggle without a license.

Kissing

There is a law in Michigan that provides that if any man kiss his wife on a Sunday, the party at fault shall be punished at the discretion of the court.

A Riverside, California, health ordinance states that two persons may not kiss without first wiping their lips with carbolized rose water.

Kite-flying

No one can fly a kite on the streets of Danbury, Connecticut, without a permit from the Mayor.

Lawn-watering

You may water your lawn on Staten Island, New York, provided you hold the hose in your hand while doing so; but to lay a hose on the lawn or to use a sprinkler for watering your lawn is unlawful.

Holyoke, Massachusetts, makes it unlawful to water your lawn when it is raining.

In York, Pennsylvania, you can't sit down while watering your lawn with a hose.

Leaning

Clinton County, Ohio, calls for a fine for anyone caught leaning against a public building.

Lemons

It is against District of Columbia law to paint lemons on your car so as to embarrass your auto dealer or any other person.

Lima, Ohio

Any map or chart on which the city of Lima, Ohio, is not prominently figured is banned from sale in that town.

Lipstick

In Pittsburgh, policewomen are not allowed to use lipstick.

Lions

Lions may not be taken to the theater in Maryland.

Loitering

Abilene, Texas, makes it illegal to idle or loiter anyplace within the corporate limits of the city for the purpose of flirting or mashing.

In Hammond, Indiana, any person who stands still and looks lazy is a loiterer.

Lollypops

It is against the law to sell lollypops in Spokane, Washington.

ᔆᔆᔆᔆᔆᔆᔆᔆᔆᔆᔆᔆᔆᔆᔆᔆᔆᔆᔆᔆᔆᔆᔆᔆᔆ

Lynchers (& Lynchees)

The Ohio General Code provides: "A person assaulted and lynched by a mob may recover, from the county in which such assault is made, a sum not to exceed five hundred dollars."

Marble-playing

Ashland, Wisconsin, forbids little boys to play marbles—if they play for keeps.

McPherson, Kansas, law forbids small boys to play marbles, "lest they acquire a taste for gambling."

Masked Balls

Dothan, Alabama, decrees it unlawful to participate in or be connected with any masked ball not authorized by the Mayor.

In New York, you have to get permission from the police before you give a masquerade.

Match-striking

In Gooding, Idaho, it is illegal to strike a match on a streetlamp post.

Mining

In Euclid, Ohio, it is unlawful to mine in your own backyard.

Monkeys

See Shoplifting

Monsters

It is against the law for a monster to enter the corporate limits of Urbana, Illinois.

Moose

Fairbanks, Alaska, has an ordinance "To keep moose off the sidewalks."

Mothers-in-law

The California Paiute Indian Reservation's laws forbid a mother-in-law to spend more than thirty days a year with her children.

Motorcycles

The town of Idaho Falls, Idaho, forbids anyone over the age of eighty-eight to ride a motorcycle.

Moustaches

Under Alabama law, the wearer of a false moustache in church who causes unseemly laughter is liable to arrest.

Ninth grade pupils in Binghamton, New York, may not sport moustaches in classrooms.

Movie Theaters

South Dakota law says it is illegal for a

theater manager to show a "whodunit," or any picture with scenes depicting illicit love, infidelity, murder or striking an officer of the law.

Owners of New York movie theaters are required by law to scrape chewing gum from under their seats at least once a month.

Mud Puddles

Michigan makes it against the law for a lady to lift her skirt more than six inches while dodging mud puddles.

In Hanford, California, people may not interfere with children jumping over water puddles.

Mules

Kentucky law holds it to be contributory negligence for a person to go behind a mule without first speaking to the animal.

In Lang, Kansas, it is against the law to drive a mule down Main Street during the month of August unless he is wearing a straw hat.

It is the law in Baltimore that any service performed by a jackass must be recorded.

Mules are protected by law in Ohio, at least to the extent that you are not allowed to ride one more than ten miles, or to set a fire under one if it balks.

In Taylor, Arizona, it is illegal for a person to kick a mule.

Murder (Attempted)

According to Virginia law, shooting and wounding a person is merely "malicious wounding," but the shooter who fires at someone else and misses altogether is charged with attempted murder.

Musical Instruments

In Boston there is a law requiring all musical instruments for use on public thoroughfares to be presented each April to the custodians of the law for examination.

Nails

Hammering a nail into a tree is punishable in Massachusetts by a fifty-dollar fine.

Newspapers

Southbridge, Massachusetts, makes it illegal to read books or newspapers after 8 P.M. in the streets.

And in Detroit, you can't sit in the middle of the street and read a newspaper.

Noses

In Leahy, Washington, men are forbidden to blow their noses in the streets, lest they frighten a horse.

Nudist Colonies

In 1934, Kentucky passed a Nudist Colony Bill providing that each such colony was to be surrounded by a fence twenty feet high and made of brick, stone or cement. Board fences were ruled out, since they might contain knot-holes. The same act provided for regular inspection of the nudists by members of the state legislature.

Onions

Princeton, Texas, makes it illegal to throw an onion.

Kirksville, Missouri, forbids frying onions

§ 80

on an open grill within a block of the city square.

Parrots

It is against the law to buy, sell, raise, or give away a parrot in the State of Georgia.

Peanuts

Massachusetts law declares that peanuts may not be eaten in court.

Peeping

In Indiana, it is illegal for a person to go anywhere "with intent to peep."

A man will not be arrested for a peeping Tom in Boston if he can show that he was spying on his wife in another man's house.

In Kansas, it is against the law for a peeping Tom to hang from a high flagstaff in order to peer into a window.

Pickles

Pickle-making, at any point within the city's jurisdiction where its aroma might offend the nostrils of passersby, is prohibited by an old Los Angeles law.

In Connecticut, it is against the law to sell pickles which, when dropped twelve inches, collapse in their own juice. "They should remain whole and even bounce."

A Trenton, New Jersey, ordinance states that it is unlawful to throw any tainted pickles in the streets.

In Central Falls, Rhode Island, it is illegal to pour pickle juice on the car tracks.

§ 82

Picnicking

It is unlawful to carry pleasure-seekers to a picnic in Indiana.

It is illegal in Nebraska to picnic twice on the same spot within any thirty-day period.

Picture Windows

In Waukegan, Illinois, you can't watch television through your neighbor's picture window.

Pigeons (Homing & Otherwise)

California law makes it a misdemeanor to detain a homing pigeon.

It is against the law for pigeons to fly over Bayonne, New Jersey, unless they are licensed.

Mobile, Alabama, says pigeon-owners are breaking the law if they allow their birds to eat pebbles from composition roofs.

Pigs

In Philadelphia, any pigs running at large without rings or yokes within fourteen miles of the navigable parts of the Delaware River can be confiscated by the Guardian of the Poor.

Pliers

Texas laws forbids anyone to have a pair of pliers in his possession.

Pockets

South Carolina law prohibits hip pockets, as furnishing a convenient place for pint bottles.

In Lexington, Kentucky, it is against the law to carry ice cream cones in your pocket.

Pop Bottles

In Tulsa, Oklahoma, you cannot open a pop bottle unless a licensed engineer is present.

Pretzels

You can't sell pretzels in Philadelphia without putting them in bags, according to an act of 1760.

Prisoners

Persons serving in the Laura, Illinois, jail are permitted to follow their trades on the outside during the day, provided they return to the jail at night.

In Denison, Iowa, it is illegal to stand at a jail window and heckle the inmates.

Winter Garden, Florida, prohibits prisoners from escaping the jail.

Privies (Academic & Otherwise)

In Ann Arbor, Michigan, a University of Michigan ordinance provides a penalty for any student, faculty member or employee who moves, tips or burns a university-owned privy.

Bexley, Ohio, prohibits slot machines in privies.

Puppets

In Warren, Idaho, puppets in Punch-and-Judy shows must wear American clothes.

Puttying

Schenectady, New York, makes it illegal to putty nail holes on Sunday.

Rabbits

In Statesville, North Carolina, a law forbids conducting rabbit races in the streets.

Radios

Citizens of Fleming, Kentucky, must not tune their radios in on any program that might offend the peace and dignity of the city.

Railroad Trains

Maryland law makes it illegal to knock a freight train off the tracks.

According to a judicial decision in New York, "A railway company which negligently throws a passenger from a crowded car on a trestle is held liable for injury to a relative who, in going to his rescue, falls through the trestle."

There is a Wisconsin law forbidding anyone but railroad employees and newspaper reporters to walk on the tracks.

It is against the law in North Dakota for a railroad engineer to take his train home with him each evening unless he carries a full crew.

See also "Wait a Minute . . ."

Rails & Tracks

Putting salt on the railroad tracks is a criminal offense in Alabama.

Rats

It is illegal to mistreat rats in Denver.

Florida law forbids rats to leave the ships docked in Tampa Bay.

Reptiles

Toledo has an ordinance that prohibits throwing reptiles at another person.

Riding

In Columbia, South Carolina, it is unlawful for women of bad character to ride horseback in the streets.

"Ring Around the Rosy"

Kansas makes it against the law to play "Ring Around the Rosy" on the Sabbath.

Roller Skates

In Portland, Oregon, it is illegal to wear roller skates in public rest rooms.

An Indiana law forbids anyone to lead young ladies astray while teaching them to roller skate.

Rumors

In Savannah, Georgia, the city code states that it is unlawful to spread false rumors.

Sauerkraut

In West Virginia, it is a penal offense to cook sauerkraut or cabbage, as the ensuing odors are common nuisances.

Schools

It is against the law to act in an obnoxious manner on the campus of a state girls' school

in South Carolina without the permission of the principal.

Seaweed

It is the law in New Hampshire that one must not gather seaweed between sunset and sunrise.

Sewers

Brockton, Massachusetts, requires persons to have a license before they are permitted to enter a sewer.

Shaving

The Morrisville, Pennsylvania, town council enacted an ordinance making it unlawful for men to shave or women to wear cosmetics if they do not have a permit.

At Poplar Bluff, Missouri, shaving during the daytime is in violation of the law.

Sheep

The law says you can't drive more than two

thousand sheep down Hollywood Boulevard at one time.

Shirts

It is against the law to go without a shirt in Toomsboro, Georgia.

Shirt Tails

In Tulsa, Oklahoma, it is illegal for a male person to walk on the streets with his shirt tail out.

Shoes & Shoelaces

North Dakota law makes it illegal for anyone to go to bed wearing shoes or boots.

In Marshall, Minnesota, women can't shine their shoes on Saturdays.

Shoplifting

A monkey once served five days in jail for shoplifting in Illinois.

Signs

Portland, Oregon, makes it against the law to parade up and down the street with a For Sale sign.

In Bloomfield, New Jersey, a child who has the whooping cough must wear a Whooping Cough sign around his or her neck.

Singing

In Boston, it is illegal to serenade beneath a lady's window late at night unless a special license is secured at City Hall.

An Oneida, Tennessee, ordinance forbids anyone to sing the song "It Ain't Goin' To Rain No Mo'."

Skeletons

In Kirksville, Missouri, it is unlawful to carry a human skeleton, or a part of one, in the public ways.

Skunks

It is illegal to put a skunk in your boss's desk in Michigan.

Sleeping

A Clawson City, Michigan, ordinance declares that villagers may sleep with their pigs, cows, goats and chickens.

Wallace, Idaho makes it unlawful for anyone to sleep in a dog kennel.

In Anderson, South Carolina, it is illegal for anyone to curl up on the railroad tracks to take a nap.

In Atlanta, it is against the law to sleep in a box on the sidewalk.

And in Lubbock, Texas, you can't sleep in a trash can.

Slingshots

Homer, Illinois, law forbids anyone but a

police officer to carry a slingshot.

In Miami, it is unlawful to carry a slingshot without a permit, or unless it is to be used lawfully in your business.

Snakes

You can't sell snakes on the street in California.

In Virginia, it is illegal to handle snakes in church.

Kansas makes it unlawful to eat snakes on Sunday.

Sneezing

You can't sneeze on the streets of Asheville, North Carolina.

It is unlawful to sneeze on a train in the State of West Virginia.

Snoring

In Upper St. Clair, Pennsylvania, anyone who snores on picket duty is not considered to be picketing peacefully.

It is against the law to snore at night in Coral Gables, Florida.

A Los Angeles judge ruled that "A private citizen may snore with immunity in his own home, even though he may be in possession of unusual and exceptional ability in that particular field."

Snow

The town of Brawley, California, passed a resolution forbidding snow within the city limits.

Snuff

It is against the law to smoke a cigarette or

use snuff in the kitchen of your home in Atlantic City, New Jersey.

Detroit law forbids playing with snuff in any hall or theater.

In Minneapolis, you can't operate a vehicle while under the influence of snuff.

Soap

Mississippi state law forbids soaping railroad tracks.

Speech

Baker, Oregon, forbids speaking to a female against her will.

And New Castle, Virginia, forbids speaking to a woman in the Post Office.

It is against the law to speak English in Illinois.

A Georgia law prohibits persons from saying "Oh, Boy" in Jonesboro.

Also in Georgia, an ordinance on the books in Flowery Branch reads: "Be it ordained, and it is hereby ordained, by the Mayor and Council of the Town . . . that on and after this date it shall be unlawful for any person or persons to holler snake within the city limits of said town."

In Spencer, Iowa, it's against the law to make personal remarks about any passerby.

Prichard, Alabama, forbids loud talking.

You can't say "delinquency" on the streets of Marcus Hook, Pennsylvania.

The speaking of any language other than the English language in any public place in the town of Sweet Home, Oregon, is prohibited.

It is unlawful to mispronounce the name of the city of Joliet, Illinois (you must say: Joe-lee-*ette*).

Sprinkling

In Longview, Washington, it is forbidden to sprinkle persons on the streets or sidewalks.

Squirrels

It is against the law to annoy squirrels in Topeka, Kansas.

Staggering

An ordinance in Opelousas, Louisiana, forbids anyone to stagger along the streets.

Street Cars

Illinois law declares that it is illegal for a streetcar conductor to collect fares without wearing a hat.

In Birmingham, Alabama, "All street car

lines are . . . prohibited from using flat wheels on their cars."

Suits

It is Texas law that any man who is picked up on the streets in dress clothes after midnight can be run in for vagrancy.

In Natoma, Kansas, it is against the law to practice knife-throwing at men wearing striped suits.

Sunflower Seeds

The eating of sunflower seeds on the streets of Endicott, Washington, or in its business houses, is prohibited.

Tattooing

In New York City, it is unlawful to tattoo a child under the age of ten.

§ 100

Taxicabs

Mobile, Alabama, says it is unlawful for a lady to ride in the front seat of a taxi if the back seat is unoccupied.

In Springfield, Massachusetts, taxi drivers are forbidden to make love in the front seats of taxicabs during working hours.

Hartford, Connecticut, decrees that carrying corpses in taxis is punishable by a five-dollar fine.

Youngstown, Ohio, makes it illegal to ride on the roof of a taxi.

Teachers

A teacher must swear that he or she has never taken part in a duel, either as a principal or as a second, before he or she is allowed to take a teaching post in Nevada.

The Montana state codes forbid abuse of

school teachers in the presence of pupils.

An old New Mexico law says that a teacher must be able to read and write English.

Tickling

It is against the law to tickle a girl in Norton, Virginia.

Tigers

In Clinton, Connecticut, no persons "shall allow their chickens, cattle or tigers to be led by chains" along the streets.

Knoxville, Tennessee, law says you must call a policeman if a tiger or lion brushes against you on the street.

Tightrope Walking

It is against the law in Omaha for circus performers to practice their tightrope walking on high-voltage lines without the proper permission.

Hammond, Indiana, law requires all tightrope walkers to be licensed.

In Winchester, Massachusetts, a young girl may not be employed to dance on a tightrope except in church.

Tobacco

In Berkeley, California, it is unlawful to smoke while fishing.

It is against the law in Newport, Rhode Island, to smoke a pipe on the street after sunset.

No person is allowed to chew tobacco without a doctor's permit in Connecticut.

And it is a misdemeanor in Sault Ste. Marie, Michigan, to expectorate against the wind.

It is illegal in the District of Columbia to flick ashes from your cigarette into the Potomac.

Toll-bridges

A California law says that a toll-gatherer may prevent from passing through his toll-gate or toll-bridge any animal that has not paid the toll.

Tombstones

In Roanoke, Virginia, it is illegal to advertise on tombstones.

In Chillicothe, Ohio, it is unlawful to place tombstones on the sidewalks.

Travel

It is illegal in Salem, West Virginia, to leave your home or dwelling without having in mind a definite place to go.

Trees

Belleville, New Jersey, says it is illegal to climb a public tree without a permit from the Shade Tree Commission.

Turtles

In Key West, Florida, turtle-racing is prohibited by law within the city limits.

Umbrellas

It is contrary to New York City law to open or close an umbrella in the presence of a horse.

Underwear

Reading, Pennsylvania, says a woman cannot hang her underwear on an outdoor clothesline unless a screen is placed around the line.

Vacuum Cleaners

In Denver it is unlawful to lend your vacuum cleaner to your next-door neighbor.

Vamping

It is against the law to vamp another woman's

husband in Adrian, Michigan.

Violin Music

In Evanston, Illinois, you are forbidden by law to give violin lessons without a license.

Augusta, Maine, makes it against the law to stroll on the street playing a violin.

"Wait a Minute . . ."

It is Texas law that when two trains meet at a railroad crossing, each shall come to a full stop, and neither shall proceed until the other has gone.

According to Arkansas law, Section 4761, Pope's Digest: "No person shall be permitted under any pretext whatever, to come nearer than fifty feet of any door or window of any polling room, from the opening of the polls until the completion of the count and the certification of the returns."

In Danville, Pennsylvania, all fire hydrants must be checked one hour before all fires.

And in Omaha, the city clerk must be notified five days before the occurrence of an injury caused by defective public ways or sidewalks, or the claimant cannot recover damages from the city.

The New York State Vehicle and Traffic Laws state that "Two vehicles which are passing each other in opposite directions shall have the right of way."

An Oklahoma law says that the driver of "any vehicle involved in an accident resulting in death . . . shall immediately stop . . . and give his name and address to the person struck."

It is the law in Pueblo, Colorado, that when two buggies approach each other in the same rut, both are required to turn to the right at the earliest practical time.

In Pocatello, Idaho, a law passed in 1912 provided that "The carrying of concealed weapons is forbidden, unless same are exhibited to public view."

By Oklahoma law, train crews must cut off the last car of each train.

Walking

It is against the law to walk on the roof of the South Carolina State House.

In Greene, New York, you cannot eat peanuts and walk backwards on the sidewalks while a concert is on.

Kansas state law requires pedestrians crossing highways at night to wear tail-lights.

It is a misdemeanor in Jacksonville, Florida, for a lady to walk on the streets without a belt.

In Devon, Connecticut, it is unlawful to walk backwards after sunset.

District of Columbia pedestrians who leap over passing autos to escape injury, and then strike the car as they come down, are liable for any damage inflicted on the vehicle.

Walking on Hands

In Hartford, Connecticut, you cannot cross the street walking on your hands.

Watermelons

Hamilton, Alabama, makes it illegal to throw watermelon seeds on the grass, sidewalks, streets or other public places.

An identical ordinance is in effect in Hammond, Indiana. There, the penalty for infringing this order is a dose of castor oil.

In Fort Wayne, Indiana, you are not allowed to carry a watermelon into a public park.

New Orleans law ordered that anyone who left a watermelon rind in a public place should be jailed.

Franklin, Tennessee, has an ordinance prohibiting the sale of watermelons.

§ 110

Water Pistols

In Louisiana, it is illegal for robbers to shoot bank tellers with water pistols.

Massachusetts makes it unlawful to duel with water pistols.

Wearing Apparel

Alton, Illinois, forbids women to wear slacks.

In Lewes, Delaware, no man may wear trousers that are form-fitting around the waist.

Phoenix, Arizona, law requires that every man wear pants when he comes to town.

Carmel, New York, has an ordinance forbidding men to wear trousers and coats that don't match.

In Chatfield, Minnesota, it is unlawful for any person to appear in the streets in dress "not belonging to his or her sex."

Wheelbarrows

In Topeka, Kansas, you may not wheel a man down the street in a wheelbarrow.

Whips

Detroit makes it a felony for a drayman to crack his whip while waiting to be hired.

Whistles

New Mexico law forbids any vehicle to be equipped with a horn or whistle that has an inharmonious sound.

A widely ignored law in Kentucky says that anyone operating a still must blow a whistle.

Whistling

Maine state law forbids whistling on Sunday.

In Vermont it is against the law to whistle under water.

Hawaii says you can't whistle in any drinking establishment.

According to Davenport, Iowa, law, it is forbidden for policemen to whistle at any girl over sixteen.

No one may whistle for his or her lost canary before 7 A.M. in Berkeley, California.

Mankato, Kansas, in 1894 passed an ordinance prohibiting the whistling and singing of "After the Ball" between the hours of 6 A.M. and 10 P.M

Whittling

An ordinance in Bremerton, Washington, forbids whittling at the foot of Pacific Avenue.

It is illegal to whittle on the streets of Tompkinsville, Kentucky.

Whooping (Etc.)

Jacksonville, Illinois, Revised Ordinances,

1884: "No person shall halloo, shout, bawl, scream, use profane language, dance, sing, whoop, quarrel, or make any unusual noise or sound in any house in such manner as to disturb the peace and quiet of the neighborhood."

Winking

The municipal code of Ottumwa, Iowa, states that "It is unlawful for any male person, within the corporate limits of the City of Ottumwa to wink at any female person with whom he is unacquainted."

Wooden Legs

The State of Delaware has a law against pawning your wooden leg.

Yo-Yo's

In Memphis, it is illegal to sell Teddy bears and yo-yo's on The Sabbath.

Index of States

Autres pays, autres mœurs—strange lands have strange customs. For the interstate traveler who wants to avoid winding at up the Bar of Justice for violating some order he knew not of, the Publisher offers this useful index. Numbers of pages on which laws from the several states appear follow state names.

§ 116